D1383360

A special thanks to Kelsey Hach for her design
magic on layouts, editing, and collaboration.
She's at: behance.net/kelseyhach

For more information or just to say "hi"
reach out to the author at:
matt@donteatthatbook.com

FIRST EDITION

ISBN: 978-1-66780-918-2

Don't

That.

Dedication...

This book is dedicated to my wife and daughters.
It's their love and support which provided the foundation for its creation.

The characters here are inspired by the first two dogs we had: Abbie and Cody.
One bossy little black dog and one big goofy white one.
These kinds of characters exist in animal shelters around the world.
Your care, kindness, and support can make a difference at any shelter in your area.

Lastly, to every kid, big or small, out there doodling, sculpting, painting, performing, imagining:
YOU ARE SPECIAL.
The world needs more art and yours makes it a better place.
Never stop doing what you love.

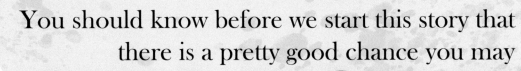

You should know before we start this story that there is a pretty good chance you may

LEARN

some stuff in here.

If you want to

STOP

and close the cover
and run away
that's totally understandable.

Alright! Way to go! I'm glad you stuck it out!
Now, before we can start this story there's something important that

PENGUINS
are from the South Pole

you have got to know.
   Penguins and polar bears are from totally different parts of the world!

POLAR BEARS
are from the North Pole

So it was quite odd when a kinda crabby penguin who loved hats...

...and an always hungry polar bear met one day...

...on the city bus where the kinda
...the always hungry polar bear reached

DON'T EAT MY HAT!

crabby penguin read a book...
for a berry on the penguin's fancy hat.

The penguin would exclaim.

But polar bears do not like yelling.
And not even the crabbiest penguins
like to see anyone sad.

So the kinda crabby penguin decided to
help the always hungry polar bear
make sure he didn't eat
anything he shouldn't
and eat ONLY the
things he
should.

There was little
doubt that the always
hungry polar bear
would need
PLENTY of help.

Don't eat that sign!

You see, you want to eat stuff that's BRIGHT and COLORFUL.

Like a rainbow but with food.

These things are good.

Carrots

Broccoli

Apples

Dumplings

Elderberries

Figs

It's broccoli. It's super good for you.
Give it a try.

Or we could try to find some other things like...

Guacamole

Hummus

Ice Cream

Look WHO'S EATING BROCCOLI

Doooon’t eeeeat thoooose jack-o-lannnterrrns!

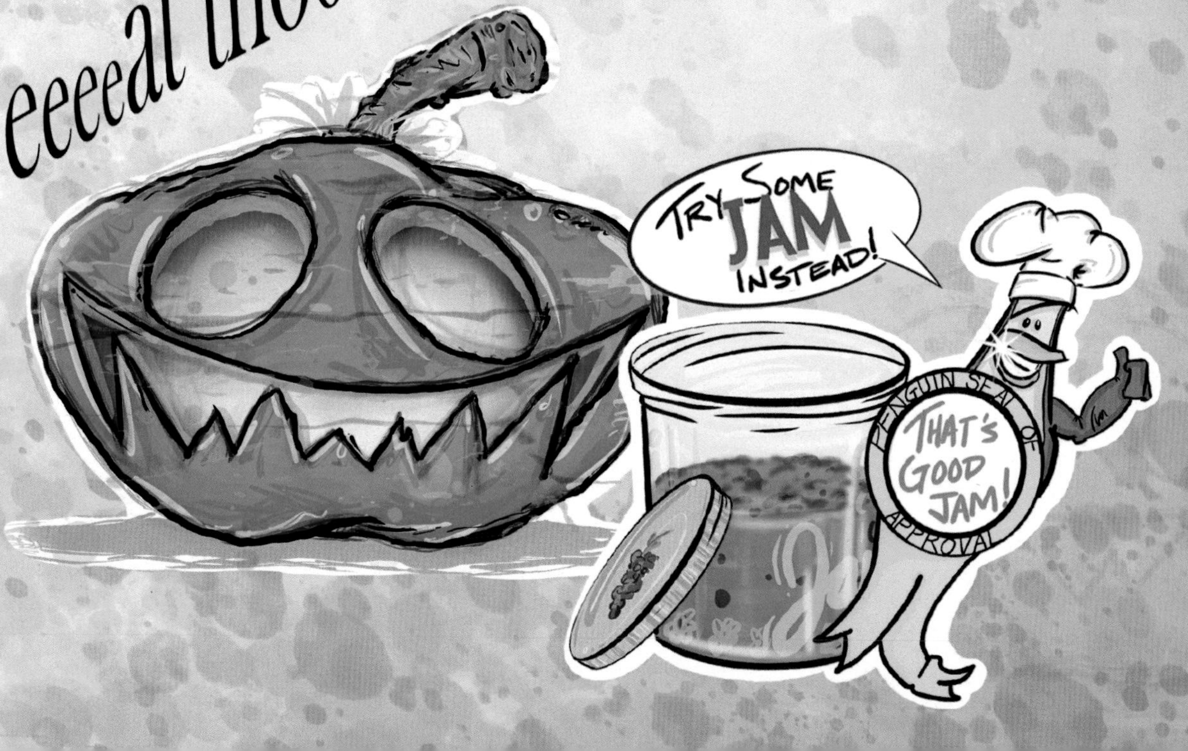

Ketchup is pretty good.

You can put it on
just about anything.

It's a little **MESSY** though.

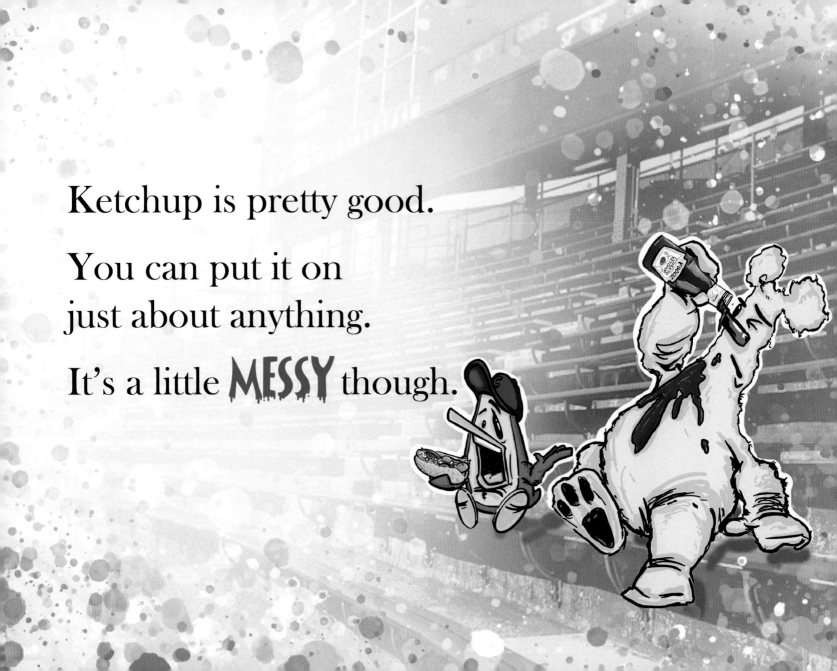

Lemons and Limes are kinds of **CITRUS**.
They can be sour, tangy, sweet or bitter.

You'll have to try them to see which you like.

Plus there's so much more, my friend!

Okra

Nectarines

Macarons

There is a whole **GALAXY** of good things
to eat out there.

Pineapples

Quince
which you say
as "kwins"
like twins

Rhubarb

Squash

Tacos are good.
You can eat them anytime.
Tacos are so good on Tuesdays
that you can SING about it!
Tacos have shells which means they
are made to go just about anywhere.
Plus, it's just fun to say "TACO"!

TACOS
I love
SO much

Umbrellas can be fun.
They are exciting to open.
You can spin an umbrella
and do a dance with your feet.
But if you are HUNGRY, it's the
umbrella fruit you should eat.

Vindaloo

Xocolatl

Which is really
just spicy hot cocoa
and is pronounced
"Sho-co-la-tl"

Watermelons

Yogurt

Zhe Fruit

Are all **GREAT** to eat and even more fun to say!

HEY!
DON'T EAT ME!

Oh.
A hug.
A hug from a friend.
The penguin realized that
he wasn't crabby anymore.
It felt **GOOD** to have
a friend.

But there was little doubt that his friend the always ~~hungry~~ huggy polar bear was still going to need PLENTY of help.

Don't hug that cactus!

Aa
Apples

Bb
Broccoli

Cc
Carrots

Dd
Dumplings

Ii
Ice Cream

Jj
Jam

Kk
Ketchup

Ll
Lemons & Limes

Mm
Macarons

Rr
Rhubarb

Ss
Squash

Tt
Tacos

Uu
Umbrella Fruit

Ee Elderberries

Ff Figs

Gg Guacamole

Hh Hummus

Nn Nectarines

Oo Okra

Pp Pineapples

Qq Quince

Vv Vindaloo

Ww Watermelons

Xx Xocolatl

Yy Yogurt

Zz Zhe Fruit

About the Author:

Matthew (Matt) Kiesling started drawing at a young age whi__
which has probably been voted "best place to learn __
a whole bunch of times. While he is still l__
also had the opportunity to learn h__
with lots of different creatur__
and po__ pe__ __cles stuck
toge__ __t the popsicle
__ make friends.

A__ __rger with two top pieces of bun and
n__ __scovered, and will probably win a prestigious award
fo__ __ch the same. Another time Matt was driving around with
__ffee and it spilled and he learned never to have a "danger beverage"
__th him or anywhere else for that matter.

MATT Lives in Lake Forest, IL
With his Amazing Wife and Kids
AND THEIR RESCUED Dogs.
He Always Finishes His Broccoli.

The author and publisher donate 100% of the profits from this book to charities
in support of growing literacy, improving health, and expanding access to the arts.